ROPED

ABBY KNOX

ROPED

BOOK FIVE IN NAUGHTY YACHTIES

Star

A job aboard a luxury charter yacht means everything to me, but I can't seem to stay focused. When my ineptitude lands me in hot water with the much older captain, I expect to be fired. Instead, the bossy Captain Joe teaches me things I never knew about myself. And now, I have a secret — that ex-Navy SEAL may run a tight ship, but underneath that tough exterior is a teddy bear that has roped me into a life I never imagined.

Captain Joe

The greenest crew member is going to be the death of me. She's so bad at her job that she's a danger to herself. Unfortunately, Star is also sweet, kind, and gorgeous, and makes me crave things I didn't know I needed. A wife. A partner. A family. Maybe it's all an illusion; maybe I've spent too much time at sea. She's a siren half my age and I don't stand a chance when her soul calls out to me. Our little secret may mean the end of my career, but it's just the beginning of my life.

ONE

Joe

LET'S get the rules out of the way first, shall we?

I am a captain, and a captain is not supposed to have feelings about his crew members. Let alone the youngest, greenest, and lowest-ranked member of the crew. I know that.

Safety first, always. Personal feelings cloud judgment, and clouded judgment sinks ships.

Acting on my feelings for my third stewardess, Star, would violate the trust built into the system. The system works. It stops working the second I betray that trust.

Here's the thing. I don't give a fuck. She already belongs to me. In my mind and in my soul, I've already claimed her as my mate. The mother of my children I never knew I wanted. My future. My whole world.

My entire body is aware of Star's breathing behind me. I don't have to look back. It's more than her scent, her sounds. And it's not the finely tuned sense of self-preservation I honed in the Navy SEALs.

Star's presence is something else entirely.

My palms sweat as I clamp them to my thighs under this dining table. As far as the royal guests are concerned, I am all in on this dinner conversation.

As the captain of the superyacht, *The Carpe Diem,* I spend a lot of time answering questions about life on a boat, about my experience in the Navy. I do it all with friendly smiles, laughter, and amusing anecdotes. I'm not exceedingly charming, but tipsy people on vacation are easily charmed.

Usually, when charter guests request the captain join them for dinner, it's a nice distraction. I enjoy donning my dress blacks and watching the sun go down with a glass of wine and a five-star meal and conversation. I'm still vigilant because often, these guests at dinner have been drinking all day, but I'm never not vigilant.

At the moment, though, all I want to do is grab the young lady behind me and drag her up to my private quarters. Explore every inch of her to figure out her secrets, understand what this hold is she has on me. Determine where that unearthly delicious scent comes from.

The royal family has no idea my mind is in two places at once. They have no idea I'm obsessed with a woman half my age. I doubt Star herself does, either. She's a young siren, and I'm an old ship in distress. She's unaware she has already annihilated me; I don't stand a chance against her magic.

The queen turns to me. "Captain, you look so familiar to me. Have we met before?"

We have met before, but I have zero interest in exploring that topic. "Yachting is a small world," I reply.

"The probability is pretty high that I've worked on a boat with you as a guest at one time or another."

The queen, thank god, accepts this answer and delicately sips her soup with a disinterested expression. The last thing I want is for Star to overhear anything about how the queen and I might have met before. Ages and ages ago, before the Navy, I'd worked on a boat with the queen, then a princess. I'd thought there was something between us, but it turned out I was simply one final fling before her arranged marriage to that pompous king that now sits across the table from me. I'd obliterated all those memories until these folks boarded the yacht earlier today.

I would hate for Star to think—what? That I'm a filthy 45-year-old boat captain lusting after his youngest and most inexperienced employee? I think my meager dating history at 18 isn't going to be the dealbreaker for Star. She'll be too busy filing a harassment lawsuit.

Shit. I need to get my head in the game.

On the outside, I ask bland questions about the king and queen's daughter's upcoming nuptials.

Inside, I am solely focused on what's happening in the background. I'm coiled so tight I'm envisioning how easy it would be for me to snatch Star away. We could disappear so fast, there would be nothing to see but overturned silver platters of beef Wellington clattering on the deck.

Right. And my esteem in the eyes of my crew—especially those who've worked with me many times before: the bosun Elijah and stews Vanessa and Juno—would go down several notches.

Star sets my plate in front of me, and I subtly glance down at her arm as it moves through my personal space. I notice the inside of her elbow, that tender skin. Her scent caresses me with a subtle hint of citrus and female musk.

I'm not hungry for fucking beef Wellington. I crave something much more delicate and further out of reach.

How would she taste? How would she look tied to my bed, wrists, and ankles tethered with rope? Would she be into it? Would she let me show her? Would she be a good girl while I devour her, or would she cry and scream my name?

Keep dreaming, old man.

As Star scurries away to fetch more wine, I watch the sway of her hips as she goes. My thumb digs painfully into my thigh, a reminder that this is the real world, and people are not characters in my fantasy.

She doesn't know, and she'll never know that she has decimated my whole sense of order with those tempting curves, shy smile, and sad eyes.

No matter where I am, what I'm doing, I can't stop thinking about her. I'm not a poetic kind of guy, but she's my North Star.

TWO

Star

I SHOULD GO.

Drop everything and run, and leave this boat far behind, Star. This crew would be better off without you.

My decision to pursue a career in yachting has put me in way over my head. I have no business being here.

I thought it would be fun to end up on the same boat as the yacht captain I've been crushing on for some time. For months, I've been setting a course to work for him. But his crew deserves better than someone entirely out of her depth.

What have I done?

And yet...

When I served the captain his main course, I felt such an insane pull toward him that I forgot who I was, where I was, what I was supposed to be doing.

I nearly allowed my fingers to pet his tousled hair.

Standing so close behind him where he dines, I saw some silver through his locks.

This wifely instinct to reach out and pet it, comb my fingers through it, kiss the top of his head, was wild. And I'd come way too close to letting my fantasy life intrude on my job.

Inside the main salon, weighed down with a tray of left-over soup bowls and empty wine decanters, I take a beat to breathe and get my bearings.

I have no business feeling what I'm feeling for my boss's boss. The captain? He's old enough to be my dad. The comparison means nothing to me in the real world; I never knew my biological father.

Age was irrelevant the instant I boarded *The Carpe Diem* a few days ago. I knew right away I was in trouble.

A tall, sun-kissed man with a beard and tousled hair watched me as I'd struggled down the dock with my luggage; no one told me I could have the big bags delivered before my arrival. So there I was, my five-foot-two frame weighed down with everything I needed for three months at sea.

He'd set down his coffee and made his way toward me to help with my bags.

I'd stumbled on the gangway when the wheel of my suitcase caught the edge of the ramp. The rolling behemoth stopped suddenly in front of me, and I'd kept going. My body flung forward, and for that split second, I thought I was about to fall into the drink or chip a tooth—neither scenario would bode well for my first day at a new career.

But then, a pair of forearms as hard as meathooks were there, catching me. Not just catching me but lifting me. I sensed my feet touching air before being set back down again.

"Are you okay?" That voice was deep and gravelly. Dark. And at that moment, I realized who he was. Judging by his age and his overall demeanor? I was looking at the captain.

No, no, I was not okay. Staring up into those haunted, beautiful blue eyes, taking in all that suntanned skin, the slight glimmer of gold in his dark, windblown hair, those deep crow's feet, grooved forehead. His hands were still on my waist, and they were big and steady as iron. Okay? No. I was weak. He looked like a mythological man who walked out of the sea: salt and wind and sun personified.

I'd blurted out words; I think I'd introduced myself. I don't know; it was all a blur. When he'd introduced himself as the captain, my hand disappeared into his two rough mitts. The handshake made me inwardly explode with warmth.

At that moment, I knew I wanted more than my hand to disappear. I wanted all of him, all over me, right away.

How would I learn the ropes of a brand new career when this man would be sharing a boat with me?

I'd consoled myself that I wouldn't have to see him all that much; he'd be on the bridge, and I'd mostly be on the interior. Slinging food and drinks, turning down beds, and cleaning toilets.

I would soon learn, though, that you can't swing a cat without hitting a crew member, even on a 150-foot superyacht. We're all in each other's faces every second, and the captain seems to be everywhere at once. He's everywhere, and yet he's so out of reach.

I look back at the dining table and watch him chat with that fancy royal family, having the time of his life.

If he knew about my silly crush, he would probably laugh in my face.

Because I'm not watching where I'm going, I run straight into Vanessa. Leftover soup splatters my chief stew all over the front of her dress.

"Shit! Star!"

My first dinner service, and I'm already a disaster.

"Oh my god, I'm so sorry. Here, let me help you!"

Vanessa trains the momentary annoyance on her face, then hands over the tray of drinks that she's somehow expertly not spilled in the collision. "No. You take this. I'll go get cleaned up."

I know she's being kind but what she doesn't know is, she's sending me back to the last place I want to be.

It takes everything in me not to make eye contact with Captain Joe for the rest of service tonight. But I have to do it to stay focused on my job and not screw up again.

Miraculously, I don't do any more damage.

At the end of my shift, after everyone has gone to bed and the sky deck is again cleared of dishes and polished, I get the call no one wants to get.

"Star, Star, Captain. Can you come to the bridge, please?"

THREE

Joe

HER APOLOGIES REACH me before she appears.

"I'm so sorry, Captain. I'm so, so, so sorry. It won't happen again, I swear."

The 21-year-old Kiwi has a lot to learn about me.

"First of all, you're not in trouble. So keep your apologies."

"I'm not, Captain?"

She's tentatively relieved, but I can't help but see the twinge of sadness in her eyes.

"Tell me how you think your day went, Star," I say.

She flinches, and her glossy lips part in a slight frown. Poor girl must think this is a discipline hearing. She thinks I'm going to shout at her the way I yell at the rest of the crew. She could not be more wrong.

"Not great, Captain. I tried. I really tried."

Star seems flustered; she could be getting ready to

confess a murder. Star is so adorable; I want to put her in my pocket. So cute, I'm almost mad about it.

"You're not in trouble. But the queen did mention an incident earlier today."

Star nods. "Yes, Captain. Vanessa asked me to get a screwdriver for the Queen, so that's what I did."

With my arms crossed in front of me, I rub the scruff of my chin to keep myself from laughing. "You gave the queen of Austero a flathead screwdriver," I say, to make sure that I understand.

Star nods. "On the silver platter, just like Vanessa said to do, with a napkin."

I can't fault her for that. She jumps whenever any of the guests or her superiors say jump. The problem is, she doesn't always know what the hell she's jumping into.

Why is she staring at my hands?

"I just wanted to make sure that you weren't a smartass," I say about the screwdriver." Star's eyes widen. "Oh, no, Captain! I wouldn't even know how to do that. I'm just tired and overwhelmed, and sometimes I'm easily confused."

"Tired? Why are you tired? Is Vanessa working you too hard? Should I talk to her?"

The stew clamps her hands over her mouth and shakes her head vigorously. "Oh no, no, no, not at all! Vanessa's a great chief stew. And Juno's been wonderful to me, too. I've been staying up late on my phone, watching YouTube videos on how to mix drinks, do a better job cleaning the shower stalls, and tie nautical knots."

My ears perk up at the last one.

"You...want to learn how to tie knots?"

"Yes, Captain. It's always fascinated me. My grandfather is a retired fisherman. When I was a little girl, he taught me a few things. I miss him so much, but I've lost all those lessons over time. So I'm trying to get them back."

"That's awfully sweet," I say, battling my internal self. I can't possibly entertain kinky thoughts about Star now that she's given me this glimpse into her life. That would be wrong.

"How about you show me which ones you remember?"

Poor, sweet, clueless Star. She lights up when I say this. "Sure, I'd love to! But I left my rope in my room."

The angel on my right shoulder whispers in my ear, *Don't do it, old man. Don't you dare go down this road.*

The devil on my left whispers, *It's just an innocent lesson in knots. Nothing unprofessional about that.*

And this is where I'm at. Bad decisions don't come out of nowhere; it starts with rationalizations.

I'm a fucking great captain. I got here by sweat and grit and taking no shit. And most importantly, respecting the rules. If my crew is not allowed to be physically involved with the guests, the boundaries between the crew and the captain are even more clearly drawn.

I'm not going to throw everything away that I believe in because of a pretty young thing who bats her eyelashes at me.

For all I know, this could be a trap.

No way am I falling for it.

FOUR

Star

THE CAPTAIN IS TRYING to sound casual, and it's cute as hell.

I may not know how to mix a margarita, tie a rope, and get easily confused when stressed, but I can read a person. Inside, the captain is jumpier than a long tail cat in a room full of rocking chairs.

"I've got some rope in here for training exercises." I watch him walk away to retrieve some rope from the storage bench along the far wall.

He's still wearing his dress blacks from dinner with the royals, and every inch of it hugs the planes and muscles of his hard body. His backside fills out the trousers so well, it leaves no doubt in my mind what those cheeks would feel like in my hands.

I know I shouldn't be thinking of my captain this way. Even if he would dare flirt with me, it could only end in heartbreak.

Still, he does a good job presenting himself as someone who would never hurt a woman. Despite all the reasons I should stop myself from going there in my mind, I know he's a good man.

Captain Joe hands me about five feet of rope, then holds out his wrists. "Show me what you got," he says.

My breath stills. I stare down at his hands, so close to my body. I can see every bump and scar on his skin, the prominent veins, the coarse hair. The thick, work-worn knuckles on those calloused fingers make me weak. I wonder what he's done with those hands. I imagine how often they've been cut, burned, pinched, or bitten by sharks. I wonder if he knows how to be gentle with those hands. If I'll ever be in a position to find out.

"Star? You okay?"

I laugh softly and shake my head, feeling heat spread across my face. "Spacing out. Sorry."

Quickly, careful not to touch his skin, I demonstrate on him the easiest knot of all, ending with a little tug that slides the loop against the skin inside his upturned wrist.

"Very good," he says. "What else do you know?"

I look away from those stormy blue eyes and tuck my hair behind my ear. "Not much else."

That's not entirely true. I've studied several kinds of knots in my late-night YouTube watching, but at the moment, I'm intimidated. I'm afraid he'll laugh at me if I do something wrong. After a full day of guests barking at me, I'm already so tender.

"Let me show you my favorite one," he says.

Something in his voice forces me to meet his gaze. Am I reading something into it, or is he...could he be trying to tell me something?

No, I decide. This is just wishful thinking having its way with me, as always.

"Okay," I say, whispering without intending to. Where is my voice? Why can't I breathe like a normal, sane, calm person? Because all the blood, oxygen, and moisture have plummeted to my sex. I am on fire for those hands, those lips, those eyes that see into my soul.

He chuckles. "You gotta let me outta this knot first."

I laugh, grateful for the release of tension. Without thinking, I allow my hand to brush against the underside of the captain's forearm. The lust is like a tidal wave. Getting a grip on my emotions, I tug the rope free as quickly as possible. He turns over his wrist and slips the rope between his fingers.

"Hold your wrists together; I'll show you a fun one," he says, his voice dropping in pitch.

Smiling nervously, I obey.

"Good girl," he murmurs. He's just old-fashioned, I tell myself. He didn't mean anything by that. He certainly didn't intend to make my thighs tremble at those words, as they are doing right now.

The captain slips the rope around my wrist, loops one end, pulls it through. His fingers move gently but firmly over my skin. "There."

The tug of rope against my skin, the brush of his fingers, the longing in his eyes. Am I dreaming, or is something happening here?

I look up from my bound wrists, trying to read what's in his eyes. I can't trust what I think I see, so blinded by the need to touch him.

I again let my inner fantasy creep to the forefront of my mind, thinking I could have his babies. I want to have them.

Right now. Starting here, on the bridge. I would if he asked me to.

My throat is dry, and I can't breathe.

Still aware of my bound wrists, I see myself circling his neck and pulling him down for a kiss. The air between us is so charged I would not be surprised to see lightning.

I flinch when he touches me again to remove the rope.

One tug, and it's gone. There's a slight burn, but I cover my wrists and smile. "Thanks; I'm not sure I can perform it from memory. Sweet of you to try to teach me. Thank you."

The captain's eyes fall to my hands. "Star, did I hurt you?"

I shake my head rapidly. "No, not at all."

Captain Joe doesn't listen to me but grasps my hands and turns them over, studying my skin. Oh, I wish he would gaze at the rest of me like that. Imagine if I was bare to him, and he was this intent and focused. I would cry, but I have no tears except those that soak my panties.

He curses. "I burned you," he says, a tremor in his voice.

"It's nothing," I say. "Doesn't hurt." I try to pull away, but he's not letting me. His fingers are strong, and he holds me tight. Oh god.

"Star. Hold still. Yes. Shit, I gave you a rope burn. Stay right here."

I want to run. I hate the idea that he thinks he's done something wrong. He hasn't. It doesn't hurt. And the dark truth is I enjoy the fact that he's left a mark on my skin.

Captain Joe has gone to his bathroom to retrieve something. He comes back with a small tub of sweet-smelling salve and applies it to my barely visible redness.

"You're too kind. I'm fine, Captain. I'm not hurt. I...um..."

As much as my body desperately craves him to

manhandle me, toss me around, bend me over the captain's chair, I am unbelievably turned on by his gentleness.

His fingers work the salve into my skin, and he may as well be petting a kitten.

Heat rushes to my face, my chest, my ears. Moisture pools between my legs. I can only imagine what an expert he would be with those fingers if all our clothes were off.

"Come back tomorrow for your next lesson."

I look up at the captain, curious. "Lesson?"

With one wink, he devastates me. "Unless you don't want me to show you the ropes."

I laugh. "I'd like to see you again," I reply. "I mean, I'd like more lessons, Captain."

I float out of the bridge and down the stairs on a high. My body buzzes with energy, my skin is warm, and everything looks different.

FIVE

Joe

I LIE AWAKE ALL NIGHT, bewildered at what's just happened.

I've never claimed anyone for myself. I never thought of anyone like that.

But I want more than just Star in my bed. For the first time in my life, I want a companion.

I never take my own wants and needs into consideration. I go back and forth all night long, wondering if this is the right thing for her. How will I tell her and not scare her away? How do I control what I really feel so she hears me out? I want to whisk her away, love her, fill her with our baby, and love her even more when her belly is round with our child.

The thought of it has my body screaming. I crave her, I want all of that, and I want it now.

But I have to wait. I have to bide my time.

The chaos of the next day keeps us apart for far too

long. I'm so tired by the end of the day that there's nothing I want more than to see Star. Alone. I want to be next to her, in the same room with her, to get a sense of normalcy. I'm anchored, but I feel untethered; I can't go to bed without seeing her.

I stare at my phone for about ten minutes, wondering if what I'm about to do is the right decision.

The mere fact that I had to look up her cell phone number in the personnel file instead of using the radio tells me that I know in my heart this is wrong.

But she did have a few more missteps today. Vanessa told me all about it.

"Don't fire her. But maybe...light a fire under her ass?"

Vanessa had no idea what she was asking.

SIX

Star

WHAT THE HECK is wrong with me?

Can I not get through a day without being alone with the captain? Without falling apart at the seams?

Without spilling a drink or making coffee that tastes like sludge?

All day he's been tied up with one thing or another. I know this in my head. But in my heart, I'm feeling flattened.

It's been another day of mistakes on my part. One of the king's guests called my coffee "rocket fuel," which I didn't realize wasn't a compliment until later when he complained to Vanessa. Then tonight, I forgot to perform turndown service. Thankfully, no one complained about that because the royal family was so out of sorts following the reveal that the princess had married Abel secretly.

Maybe seeing Abel fall in love worked its way into my heart. On the one hand, I am happy for him. On the other hand, I may never have that.

The captain is just toying with me. Or maybe he's not. Perhaps he's completely innocent, and I'm reading into every word he says.

After I clock out, I sit on the bottom step of the winding staircase that leads up to the bridge. I just sit there in my sadness. What was I expecting from him? A "good morning" text? A "come see me" text in the middle of the afternoon?

He's not toying; he's swamped. And I'm a pathetic, needy young girl who needs too much. He can't give me what I want, and I shouldn't expect anything from him.

Tears run down my face, and I don't wipe them away. I let them flow, and I allow myself to feel sad, assuming I'm alone. Everyone has finally gone to bed.

Or so I thought.

Dustin picks the worst moments to talk to me.

"Hey, what's wrong, honey?"

I bristle at this.

Wiping the wetness from my cheek, I ask him, "Please don't call me that. My name's Star."

He squats down, so he's right in front of me. "You can talk to Uncle Dustin."

If this doesn't prove that age is just a number, I don't know what is. For someone my age, Dustin is giving dirty old man vibes. "That's maybe the creepiest way to attempt to get to know me."

He chuckles. "Funny, I thought you liked father figures."

I sit up straight and look at him. "What?"

My phone pings in my pocket. Saved by the bell. Dustin stands there as I unlock my screen, so I glare up at him. "Do you mind?"

He slowly backs away, and I instantly forget the entire

conversation because the words on my screen cancel out every tear I had been shedding just a minute ago.

"Come up for another knot tying lesson when you're finished with your shift," the text reads.

Oh my god, oh my god, oh my god.

Seconds later, I'm alone with the captain on the bridge, and he's already got the same length of rope in one hand.

I wonder if we're going to skate around the issue again, have another flirting session under the pretense of learning how to tie knots. I don't know if my heart can handle the coyness anymore.

My eyes go to the captain's hands, which fiddle with the rope. I watch its length slide through his closed fist as he talks, wishing that was me he was caressing, manipulating, thoughtlessly messing with. I am weak.

"Star," he starts, with a certain edge in his voice that makes my eyes snap to his.

"Yes?"

"I have to tell you something before we take these... lessons...any further. I need you to know something. I'm not motivated by your desire to learn knots. I'm motivated solely by my own ulterior motives."

I wait for a beat, and I feel the air between us thick with heat like the summer night outside. There's a storm coming, and it crackles under my skin. Touch me, I want to say. Move me. Have your way with me. With a trembling voice, I ask, "What motives?"

I hold my breath. I'll breathe again if he says what I want him to say. He could say nothing and simply reach out his hands to fist my hair, rip off my clothes, cup my breasts, breathe against the skin of my chest, and I'd be his. Instantly. Completely. If he says we have to stop meeting like this, that this is inappropriate, or I've misread his feelings, I will never breathe again.

The radio crackles; Juno is calling me.

The sound of my superior's voice jars me back to reality. What am I doing? Everything we're about to do—or what I think we're about to do—compromises this boat's entire chain of command. None of this flirtation is fair to my coworkers. It takes the focus off of what we're doing here. We're here to work, not mess around with each other.

"I should go," I say.

"Star. Wait."

This is messed up. I turn and sprint off the bridge and down to the galley, where Juno is calling me to finish up washing dishes.

Knot tying lessons, my ass. This is turning into something else, and it will mean trouble for everyone.

GLASS SHATTERS EVERYWHERE. An epic amount of it.

Juno might burst a blood vessel.

"We literally have no champagne glasses left, Star," she says.

My heart beats outside of my chest.

I look around me, and the mess of shattered bits of glass and champagne glitters in the sunlight, creating a chaotic sparkle across the wood. It would be pretty if it weren't so dangerous. That's right. We're now on our second charter of the season, and I've managed to stay away from being alone with the captain. And he's respected my boundaries, dammit.

I'm so distracted by my own wishful thinking that I'm

making mistakes right and left. And the barefoot primary is about to step right into it.

Ian. Vanessa's Ian.

I jump into action, leaping over the broken glass with no regard for myself. Aiming to block Ian from injuring himself, I knock the man right on his ass.

"Whoa!" Ian yelps.

While Andre helps Ian to his feet, Juno has already set up the warning signs around the area to ward off anyone else.

Glaring at me, she hands me the broom, then brushes past me.

"I'm so sorry."

She grimaces. "It's not me you have to worry about. You might want to watch out for hormonal Vanessa."

I don't have time to ask what she means because Vanessa is standing right behind her.

Juno squints at me. "She's right behind me, isn't she?"

"Kind of."

I watch Vanessa turn around and go straight up the stairs to the bridge, and I'm left to clean up the mess I made.

Andre very kindly helps me clear the floor of glass, and then I mop up the sticky liquid while Juno fetches the trash can. A few minutes later, Andre and I are alone, going over the surface of the teak, again and again, making sure we haven't missed a single shard.

Always the kindest deckhand on this vessel, Andre makes a joke. "That's one way to get guests to drink less," he says.

At first, this provokes a chuckle from me. But the comic relief morphs into something else: a release valve.

I'm not chuckling; I'm crying. I can't stop myself; the tears are coming and coming, and then the sobbing.

"Honey, what is wrong?"

Thank god this outburst is happening in front of Andre and not Juno or Juliet. Both have seen me cry enough that they'd probably prefer to slap me than comfort me.

"I'm so tired of fucking up," I say, my breath shuddering. Great, my nose is running now.

He gives me a sideways, brotherly squeeze. "Hey. It's fine. Everything is going to be fine."

What if this nice man knew about my feelings for the captain? What if he knew the captain has been kind of, sort of flirting with me? He would rightly tell Elijah, who would go straight to the yacht owner. The captain could be disciplined or fired. And if he wasn't removed from the boat, there could be a mass exodus of the crew in protest. At the very least, everyone would lose respect for Captain Joe. I can't have any of this on my conscience.

Fully choking sobs spew forth. Nothing is going to be okay. Vanessa is on the bridge now, demanding that Captain Joe fire me. I know this with one hundred percent certainty. I would deserve to be let go for what I did.

"A little bit of broken glass is not worth tears," Andre says.

He's right, but I'm not crying over the glass.

Vanessa returns from her meeting with the captain, looking a little queasy. She says nothing to me except, "Well, I suppose I'd better order new champagne glasses."

She's trying to sound breezy, but I know she's anything but.

When I'm called up to the bridge, Andre wishes me luck. I turn and nod blandly, but my insides are roiling.

I don't know if this is a good thing or a bad thing. I can't seem to pin down my emotions.

Up the steps to the bridge, I can't even imagine what

awaits me at the top. We left things—I left things—unfinished the last time we were alone together, over a week ago.

I've been a mess ever since. Holding in a secret and denying myself any resolution to the "he likes me/he likes me not."

Everything—all of my twisted emotions, inhibitions, regret, fear—go by the wayside the second I see Captain Joe's face.

He's standing there, feet planted, arms folded across his chest, waiting. He has a look of determination.

I take a deep breath and prepare myself to be disciplined. Disciplined, or faced with finishing the conversation that I had abruptly cut off last week when he had been trying to tell me about his "ulterior motives."

Or, perhaps, I'll simply be taught a new knot-tying technique.

I don't know which end result of this meeting I fear the most.

SEVEN

Joe

"YES, CAPTAIN."

Star looks like a lamb being led to the slaughter.

I can't let this torment continue.

"You can just call me Joe."

She blinks up at me, surprised. "That's not what Vanessa told me. That's also not okay, according to the Maritime Handbook—"

"Fuck the Handbook."

"Okay."

I don't think. I don't question the force that compels me forward. I just act.

The distance between us closes. Scooping this little beauty up into my arms, we kiss. I kiss her with everything in me. She kisses me, and my heart explodes. Her soft, ardent moans are met with my sighing groan of relief.

Shit, kissing her is as good as I knew it would be. Better, even.

This past week has been torture. I've been giving her the space that she needed. Even though we'd left things unspoken at our last meeting, she knew what I was trying to say. Somewhere inside, she knew, and she couldn't deal. I wanted to respect her need to process. I tried and failed every night to put her out of my mind so I could focus on my job. But every night, I closed my eyes and saw her face. I saw my heart and soul just out of reach, and no amount of self-induced physical relief could help my sorry state.

Now, I have her. As wrong as it is, it feels right. She's everything. She's my bright star in the sky, and I'm never taking my eyes off her again.

"This feels naughty," she says, pulling away from the kiss. "Get it? Naughty. Knotty."

Marry me, you corny little thing. Marry me right now. Absentmindedly I tuck a flyaway lock of her hair behind her ear. "Can I keep you?"

Without a second thought, she nods. "Yes," she answers breathily.

EIGHT

Star

HIS LIPS MOVE over mine in a sensuous kiss, and my world as I know it is redefined.

The kiss is everything I thought it would be; Captain Joe kisses like he means it. Just like everything he does and everything he says. He knows what he's doing.

I want a deeper kiss, and he knows it. His strong arms tighten around my waist, and my feet come up off the ground. Should I be concerned that I can't run away because he's holding me captive in his arms as if I weigh no more than a sack of potatoes? Maybe I should, but I don't care.

The kissing is too good. His big hands on the small of my back are too perfect. The closeness is like a blanket, blocking out all our problems. Maybe this is deluded, but I don't care.

Captain Joe's warm tongue swipes against the seam of my lips, and I open to him. Our tongues meet, ratcheting up my desire tenfold. This hot, slow, deep, brain-melting kiss could last for days, and I would not mind. We could get caught right now, and I would not mind. My entire body roars to life as if someone pulled the cord on all my engines. My skin tingles from my scalp down to my toes. My nipples harden at the friction of our bodies.

The captain's rigid cock twitches against my leg. I gasp against his mouth at the sensation of that erection. The fact that I've done that to him—that little ol' me could inspire such a thing—drives me insane for him.

I scrape my fingertips through that soft, tousled hair as our tongues and breath tangle. He tastes minty like he'd recently brushed. Had he been preparing for this? Thinking about kissing me? The fact that this man—this towering, intimidating, legendary, accomplished captain that takes zero shit from anyone—would brush his teeth in hopes that I might want to kiss him is just too much to wrap my head around. What even am I, in the presence of this man? I'm nothing but a bumbling, clueless, green third stew who is routinely banished to the laundry room. And now? I'm an object of his desire. Am I okay with being an object?

His lips brush over my chin and down my neck, where he kisses and nibbles in a most sensitive spot. Heat surges through me, compelling me to climb. To where? I don't know, but my legs want to wrap around him. My thighs simply must own him. My soaking wet core wants to mark his crisply ironed trousers like a stamp.

The answer to my question is yes. At this moment, I am more than okay with being an object of simple, depraved lust. It is broad daylight, and I will scramble up his body and ride him.

Without pausing his ministrations to my neck, the captain yanks roughly at one of my scrabbling legs, hooking it around his waist. He does the same to the other, and I'm fully clinging to him. And we're moving.

The next thing I know, we're backed up against something. I don't know what it is, but it doesn't really matter because again, he's kissing me. Annihilating me with his mouth, so fiercely plunging his tongue into me that I can't breathe. And I don't care. I want more. I want him to breathe for me. That's a thing, right?

His hands. Oh god, those big, rough hands have jerked my uniform polo out of my khakis, giving him access to the bare skin of my back. The delight I feel as he caresses and scrapes makes me moan urgently into his mouth. My pelvis grinds against his middle, urging him on. One hand steadies us against the wall, and the other moves from my back to my ass, dragging and tugging. Oh god, he's undressing me. Am I okay with this? Yes, yes, a thousand times yes. I need more skin against my skin, more contact. More everything.

I can't wriggle out of these shorts while clinging to him. He realizes this too and drags us over to the captain's chair, where he sets me down and works frantically at my button and zipper. Arcing upwards, I help him tug down my shorts past my knees, and the next thing I know, he's cupping my pussy.

My body jerks at the contact, my breath gasping, absorbing his groans at the feel of my wetness against his fingers.

I am bare-ass naked from the waist down, dripping all over the leather chair where this great man sits. It may as well be a throne, and look what I'm doing to it. What he's making me do.

He knows it, and he doesn't care. His calloused fingers root around between my folds, the obscene wet sounds making me blush.

He pulls away from our kiss to study my face while exploring my pussy. "That's my girl."

My head nearly explodes. No one has ever touched me like this before, called me that, or...made me feel any of these things.

But I'm so in the moment, I just start blurting words. "Yes, Daddy."

This was evidently the right thing to say because his growl comes from somewhere deep in his chest. No, that's not right. It comes from somewhere deeper and darker and totally uncivilized.

The fire inside me thrums. The captain sinks a thick finger inside, and I bite down on my lip, stifling a moan. I close my eyes, overcome by these new experiences, my mind hurtling to catch up with what my body is experiencing.

"Open your eyes, Sunshine."

I obey, and when I do, I see him adjust himself. My god, I may drool on myself. The bulge is long but also thick. Of course, it is; the man embodies big dick energy.

He sees me looking, and his gaze grows more intense. He looks like a wolf, and he's about to eat me alive. I watch his jaw tic as his thumb finds my clit. I let out an embarrassing squeak and fist his shirt, and his eyes grow fiercer.

Again he's kissing me, and I melt into his touch. My body presses back against the plunging of his finger inside me. He adds a second as his thumb circles my clit.

I'm writhing under him, wishing I could hug him with my legs, except my shorts are still wrapped around my ankles. He seems to like it that way; he likes me somewhat restrained. Honestly, so do I.

It doesn't take long before his caressing, massaging, and circling of my clit has me breaking apart at the seams. I've never orgasmed before, so I'm not prepared for the noises I make. Something like a yelp and a grunt. To me, it's embarrassing, but the captain only smiles wolfishly, satisfied with what he's done to me.

"Good girl. Such a good girl."

His words, kisses, and relentless fingers pull every last involuntary spasm out of me. I'm left breathless, spent, shocked at what he's just done to me.

I barely notice him putting me back together until I'm upright if leaning against his chest, my polo tucked neatly into my khaki shorts.

I'm suddenly horrified at the realization that I just came all over the captain's chair. I pull away from him, but he slams me back against his chest. "Where you goin'?"

"I...I need to clean up. Um. Your chair? Oh god, don't make me say it."

The kiss this time is warm and tender. Restrained, but sweet. "Don't you dare."

"I've, uh, cleaned up much worse before. You should see the things people do in the guest cabins."

Ever so slightly, Captain Joe narrows his eyes at me. Is it judgment? Is he about to reject me? Has he had enough of me?

He quickly dispels my doubts by cupping one half of my face with one of those big hands and murmuring directly in my ear. "You're mine. I want your scent, your mark, all over everything. When I tell you not to clean up after yourself, you'd better fucking listen, little girl. Do you understand me?"

With a trembling breath, I answer him. "Yes, Captain."

Once again, he's hoisting me up, kissing me again and again.

And still, there's his hard length, which seems to have

grown in the time since I first noticed it. I want to touch it, rub it, take it out and give him some relief. Really, Star? And what would you do with a great big Navy SEAL cock if you did take it out?

That's varsity level sexual prowess, and you're a freshman.

That's when I start to panic.

This is a man more than 20 years older than me. What am I doing? He will not be impressed by anything once the making out moves on to hotter and heavier things.

I have to press pause. I have to get out of here and rethink.

I have to tell him the truth.

As much as I want to keep kissing him, I know that's not where things can stay for much longer.

Squirming in his arms, I force myself to pull away.

He looks at me like I've jabbed a knife into his heart.

"Wait. Stop. Put me down."

NINE

Joe

ONE MINUTE I've got my sunshine in my arms. The next minute she's wriggling to get away.

Of course, I immediately set her down because every movement, every squirm against me, only gets me more rigid.

"I'm sorry, we can stop for now," I say.

Star looks up at me, sadness once again filling her eyes. "We may need to stop for good after telling you what I have to tell you."

Okay, what did I do wrong? Is she hurt? Am I a terrible kisser? Is my breath bad? Did she decide I'm too old after all? After getting a taste of the old man, is she changing her mind? God, I wouldn't blame her. All these thoughts race through my mind as I prepare myself to be okay with whatever she's about to tell me.

"Did I do something? Did I hurt you?"

Star shakes her head, breathing heavily.

"No, you didn't do anything wrong. I did."

I can't fathom anything she might have done wrong. "I doubt that very much."

She blurts out, "I'm a virgin."

I take a beat, mostly because I'm waiting for her to add to that.

But nothing else comes.

"That's it?"

She shakes her head again. "You don't care that I'm a virgin?"

"Doesn't matter to me if you are or you ain't a virgin, Sunshine."

"Are you just saying that to make me feel better?"

Gently, I grind against her just to get the point across. "Does it feel to you like it matters?"

Her eyes widen, her lips fall open in shock; my aching cock has only gotten harder in the time that our bodies weren't touching.

"Oh. Oh my..."

"I want you in my bed. Tonight. Don't go to your cabin. You're with me now. And when I wake up in the morning, and you've left for breakfast service, your scent better be all over me and the sheets."

A pink hue floods her cheeks, her throat bobs.

"But before this goes any further, you need to know something. I've been thinking about this a lot, and I need to be upfront about it. I've known about this for a while, but it didn't crystalize until I met you. I want a wife. I want babies. I want a family to care for and protect. Taking care of a crew and these boats is not enough anymore. I want someone in my corner, and I want to build something. Over the past week, I decided. I want you, and I want you to give me all the things I've been missing in my life. And I want to start now."

This is it. She's either going to run screaming, or she's into this idea.

She bites her swollen bottom lip. "Captain. As soon as you touched me...the first time I saw your face, I knew. Something in me was scratching to get out; I wanted to have a hundred babies with you right away."

I laugh, both in relief and amusement, at the idea of a hundred of our babies running around. My guiding star, my lucky star, call this whatever you want, but it's destiny. I found the one.

TEN

♡

Star

I DON'T KNOW if I missed Vanessa's surprise pregnancy because I just don't know the symptoms or if I've been too distracted by the captain.

It must be the latter because I've apparently also missed that Ian is the father. The only reason he's here—alone, the sole guest on this charter—is because he moved heaven and earth to find her after their one-night stand in Monaco.

"I feel like I didn't even have the chance to prove myself to you," I tell Vanessa as we hug goodbye on the dock. I've barely worked with her for two weeks, and I already feel attached. She was so kind and patient with me, even when banishing me to the laundry.

Vanessa smiles and gently pinches my cheek. "You don't have to prove anything to me. Besides, Juno will whip you into shape."

Juno cackles. "I've got bigger fish to fry in the kitchen. You'll do fine," she says.

Juno has me hopping to turn the boat over for the next charter as soon as she's gone. Since we only had a single guest who barely caused a fuss this time, most of the ship is still clean.

Nevertheless, Juno has me mopping and polishing every surface of the interior.

"Leave the kitchen and pantry area to me. I have to meet with Maksim to plan the next charter anyway."

I don't know why she says that so stiffly, like planning out the menu with Maksim would be such a chore. From what I've noticed, she seems to enjoy verbally sparring with him.

After a full day of cleaning the boat, the captain makes a special announcement that gets everyone excited. Everyone except me.

"Good news, everyone. With Ian departing early and leaving you guys a huge-ass tip, you have some time before the next charter to relax. I've booked you all two nights at a beach resort in Naples, and that's an order."

While everyone cheers, my heart sinks.

I was supposed to spend the night in the captain's quarters, and now he's sending the rest of the crew and me away?

Maybe he's changed his mind about me.

If that's the case, no amount of beach time in the Mediterranean will make me feel better.

While showering off the day's hard work, I go over everything I did and everything I said this morning while he was kissing me on the bridge. Maybe he is actually having second thoughts about me being a virgin. Maybe in the hours we've been apart, he's had time to think about all the insane things we declared to each other.

The text from him comes in while I'm packing my suitcase for the trip ashore. "Tell them you feel like you've got a stomach bug."

It takes me a second, but then I figure it out. The captain has bought us two nights entirely alone without any of the crew on board.

"IT FEELS nice to kiss you out in the open air."

I say this as Captain Joe, and I are on a private balcony in a sumptuous hotel room in the heart of the city.

As soon as the crew left for the resort, the captain whisked me away to a casual dinner at an outdoor cafe. After dinner, we walked the charming streets, ate gelato, and took in a movie.

We watched part of the movie until the captain saw me nodding off.

He'd sighed and then sweetly cupped my cheek, kissing my forehead. "My Sunshine had a long day. Let's go."

For a man who worked so hard at being discreet around the crew, he certainly didn't care about making a spectacle in the middle of downtown. He'd scooped me up in his arms and carried me straight to the hotel.

"I'm fine to walk. I'm not that tired."

He'd murmured in my ear, ignoring passersby's comments and amused looks, "I'm saving your energy."

A thrill rushed through me at his words and his lips against my ear.

I sigh. "I don't know if I'll be much fun tonight. I'm exhausted."

He laughs wickedly as we pass through the door to the hotel suite, and he carefully lays me on the bed.

"You don't have to do anything but take off those clothes and let me see you," he says.

Shuffling out of my dress, I should feel self-conscious. But watching him watch me blots out any reservations. I peel off my underwear and bra, tossing them on the chair with my dress.

"Look at my girl. Look at you."

I watch open-mouthed as the captain unzips, adjusts, and partially tugs his cock from his boxer briefs. Dark pink and veiny, the part of it I can see twitches when my eyes land on it.

He's...going to put that whole thing...inside me?

I can do this. I'm ready. Put me in, coach; I'm ready to play.

Captain Joe crouches over me on the bed and worships my breasts. Wetness instantly pools in my sex, and I involuntarily mewl like a kitten.

"I...I'm not sure how to do this," I whisper, blushing deeply.

He reaches down and picks up one wrist and kisses the tender skin on the inside of it. He repeats this with the other and says, "All you have to do is be a good girl while I show you a couple of my favorite knots."

Ho. Lee. Shit.

ELEVEN

Joe

"YES, CAPTAIN."

There's nothing left to say.

It's all I can do to restrain the urge to pounce on her, ravage her, as I secure her wrists to the headboard. Yes, I brought two lengths of rope. Yes, I had every intention of using them precisely like this.

Once my Sunshine is fastened down securely, I look over every inch of her.

How did I get so lucky? My Star. My siren. My everything.

I go slow, slower than I want to, covering her with kisses. I leave nothing untouched, untasted, except for one wicked little spot.

After our interlude on the bridge this morning, her scent on my hands, in my chair has driven me insane. I knew I had to get her away from the prying eyes of the crew.

I'm so glad I waited for this opportunity.

Her nipples pebble in my mouth, and she moans as I suckle each one. Star's skin glows like starlight, and it's so soft. So young and soft and supple against my hardness. It's truly a wonder that she'd give herself like this to a crass old sailor with a one-track mind.

I kiss my way back up to eye level to check in. "If you want to stop, if you want out of these ropes, you tell me."

She nods, her chest rising and falling rapidly with her breathing. "Don't you know every time you bound my wrists together, it got me wet?"

This catches me off guard.

"Oh, but why are you surprised? Every time you do what you want with me, I swear I'm like a fountain."

I can barely describe what it feels like to hear her say these words. "My shy little Star is so naughty."

She pouts. "You made me do it. And now you'll have to punish me."

My breath catches. She's got me speechless.

"Please, Daddy?"

Her wantonness pulls an involuntary growl out of me. Holy fuck.

My innocent girl has transformed into a sex goddess before my eyes. Who is this woman, and where did she come from? Aside from straight out of the sea's murky depths to suck me down under into oblivion.

I'm going down into nothingness, taking her with me.

Knocking her knees apart, I paint kisses down the inside of her thigh and back up the other side until I'm at her core.

She's already sticky with her sweetness. When I press my lips against hers, I'm instantly hooked on her essence, which tastes like warm honey on my tongue. Her back arches off the bed at the contact.

But I'm far from done. I devour her with my teasing lips

and tongue, splitting her open with my thumbs to drink in more. I close my lips over her taut little clit, and she shudders beneath me in her first release.

Her arms flex, her wrists tight against the ropes. "Oh my god! Oh my god!" The headboard creaks in protest against her surprising strength.

I skim my hands over her soft tummy, her squeezable cheeks, kissing every spot I can reach until she finishes.

"I want to touch you, Captain!"

"Not yet, Sunshine."

I share her taste with her mouth, her gasping breath wafting over my face.

"Okay," she says.

"Good girl."

Her eyes roam over my body as I stand and drop my trousers and rid myself of the rest of my clothes. I'm overcome when I see her pink tongue slip out to lick her lips in response to the full view of my dick. "I've never seen one before. I've never touched one. I don't...I'm not sure what to do with it."

Hovering over her again, I shush her with my mouth. "I said, you don't have to do anything but take me. You ready?"

She nods. Every inch of her is flushed. I take a mental picture; I never want to forget how she looks at this moment.

With our eyes locked on each other, I hoist her hips upward and notch my cock inside her warmth.

Her lips part, her eyes widen as I push in, inch by inch.

"Good?"

She nods. "Good. Keep going."

I wait briefly for her muscles to adjust to my size. Her heat is almost too much, and it takes every ounce of discipline in me not to nut right now.

Deeper and deeper, I push inside her heat until I'm fully seated.

Something comes over me, and instead of thrusting as madly as I'd like to, I have to tell her something.

"Star. I love you."

"You do?"

Smirking, I reply, "Probably a good idea to start with that since I'm planning on getting you pregnant."

She laughs, and the sound of her vibrates through me. "I lied," she says.

Setting aside the fact that I'm buried inside her at the moment, I have to investigate now. "About what?"

Biting down on her pouty bottom lip, she answers, "I lied about when I knew I wanted to have your babies."

"Oh?"

"I was saving myself for a boat captain. Specifically, that's why I got into this job. I did some research, and I found you. And I sort of...made sure that they'd assign me to your crew when the agency hired me. I didn't want to work for anyone but you. I know everything about you, and I loved you from day one. I've been waiting to meet you for months."

"Star," I choke out.

I'm so shocked that I forget she's tethered to the bed; I hug her around her waist and try to roll her on top of me. Only when she yelps in pain do I realize what I've done.

"Sunshine! Oh shit, I'm sorry."

She laughs. "I'm okay!"

I work loose both knots frantically and then look her over for injuries. "I just wanted you to have a good first experience, and instead, I hurt you. Look what I did!"

"Really, it's nothing. I don't feel anything," she insists.

"Stop being so nice and let me get the aloe vera."

Instead, Star clamps her legs around me and draws me back in. Harder than I thought would be possible for her.

I chuckle. "You've got strong legs."

She seethes at me, the muscles of her sex clamping down around me so tight I may fold in on myself. "Don't. You. Dare. Leave."

What choice do I have? "Yes, ma'am."

I drive into her; her mouth slackens. "Yes, please, more," she hisses.

She's so damn tight, claiming every inch of me. She's not my guiding star; now, she's my superstar.

My goddess.

"I can't believe you stalked me. My girl stalked me and found me." I pull out and drive into her again, and she moans, digging her nails into my back.

Continuing our grinding, I marvel between grunts and curses in my overwhelming pleasure in her.

"I thought I claimed you first, but you sought me out. Such a dirty, naughty girl. I'm so fucking lucky. So lucky."

She's wild tonight, full of energy she didn't have earlier this evening. "Ride me, Star."

"Yes, please."

I roll her over until she's on top of me, impaled on my dick. Right where she belongs.

"Tell me what to do, Captain."

Reaching down, I weave our fingers together and pull her down for a kiss. "Just hang on; that's all you have to do."

I continue to pierce her, obliterating all space between us. We move together, grinding, slapping, bouncing until we're dripping with sweat. When I'm close, I reach down between us and thumb her clit, which is tight with needing to be touched.

"Yes, Captain. Oh god, yes!"

Her moans and cries push me over the edge until I'm exploding my release inside her beautiful cunt.

Simultaneously I curse and praise her, my seed surging inside her warmth, exactly where it needs to be.

I come, and I come, and I come some more. How am I so hard? How was I that full of cum? Every thrust upward releases more of me, and she takes all of it.

She breaks apart in another release, shouting my name. "Joe!"

Not my title. Not her bedroom nickname for me. My name.

"Star."

Breathless and somewhat startled at what just happened, I hug her close, burying my face in her hair. I want her all over me, as often and thoroughly as possible.

I was correct to say, "fuck the rules." I feel no shame. I feel more whole than I've ever felt in my entire life.

TWELVE

Star

BEING BANISHED to the solo grunt work on *The Carpe Diem* can't affect me anymore.

None of that bothered me much before, to be honest. I was always happy to do my part. But now, with everything that's happened, no negativity can touch me.

Even being left alone to wash the dishes until one a.m. can't affect me.

Until Dustin shows up. We're now well into the next charter of the season, serving a group of Instagram influencers. Everyone finally went to bed after midnight, and I had thought I was alone in the galley.

"What did you and the captain get up to while we were on our break?"

I nearly jump out of my skin and drop a crystal wine glass in the sink, shattering it to pieces.

"Shit!"

"Easy," Dustin croons. "Nothing to be jumpy about. It

was a simple question. Your poor stomach must have really been in knots, seeing as you never showed up to the resort."

Stomach. Knots. That choice of word is purely coincidental. It has to be.

I snap, "How about you get me something to clean this up with? And try not to sneak up on people?"

Dustin obliges, but only after reminding me that he outranks me and I can't boss him around like that.

"I don't report to you. I report to Juno. She would tell you the same thing."

Dustin's narrowed eyes track on something that makes his mouth go slack.

"Oh my god," he says. His face turns three shades of white and then green. He bolts, and I'm left confused.

It's then that I feel the warm sensation on my hands. Blood drips down into the soapy water, and I'm alone.

THIRTEEN

Joe

STAR DIDN'T COME to my cabin last night, and I'm losing it.

I'd seen how rowdy those guests were, and I'd stayed awake to keep an eye on them for as long as possible. The law requires me to get adequate sleep for safety reasons. I tried to push it, but Star, Juno, and our new stew Juliet insisted that I let the interior crew handle the guests.

Star had texted me about two a.m., saying she was exhausted and wanted to sleep. That's probably for the best. We don't get much sleep when we're together.

But now it's nine a.m., and I haven't seen Star all morning.

Juno brings me my coffee on the bridge. I can't figure out a good reason to ask about Star, so I ask some stupidly bland questions about how the changes are going with the interior crew.

Juno grimaces. "Juliet's great. Star? Still could use some work."

The coffee mug warms my hands as I drink it down. "What do you mean?"

"She cut herself washing dishes last night, so I put her on laundry. I can't have her serving guests or handling food when her hands are covered in bandages."

I sit up straight. "What the hell happened?"

Vanessa shook her head. "All she said was something startled her, and she dropped a goblet in the sink, and it broke."

Forgetting about my coffee, I brush past Juno.

"Captain?"

"I have to check on her and make sure she's okay."

"Oh. Yes, of course, Captain."

I find Star in the laundry room, ironing my black trousers from last night.

"There you are."

My voice is too intense, too emotional, but I don't care.

Star looks up, startled. "Captain!"

I look down at her hands and see the bandages. It's not as bad as I had pictured in my mind, but I'm gripped by my idiotic decision to leave her alone last night.

"Why don't you put down that iron and tell me what happened?"

She nibbles on her bottom lip nervously. "I'm so sorry. I dropped a glass, and it broke, and some glass cut me and...."

"Show me."

She blushes and shakes her head. "It's nothing; I'll be fine."

Before she can say another word, I've shoved the ironing board out of the way, not caring about my clothes, the hot iron. I hate that she's injured and that she's minimizing it.

I take her wrists in my hands and examine the bandages. "Who did this to you?"

"Nobody! It was nothing, I—Dustin came up behind me, and I got startled."

"Dustin," I growl.

Star continues to protest. "No, no, he didn't do anything. Please don't be upset with him."

I'm already unwrapping the bandages and examining her wounds. A few minor scrapes and two or three deeper flesh wounds have already begun to heal. I sigh in relief.

"Who bandaged you up? If it was Dustin, I'll fucking kill him. This is a half-assed job. He should have taken you to see the medic right away."

She shakes her head. "It was me. He didn't know I'd hurt myself. I was alone, and I had to fix myself up. It didn't even hurt."

My stomach rolls over at the thought of her being hurt and alone and trying to wrap up her own wounds.

"Jesus," I grit out. "Come on. Up to the bridge."

"B-but your clothes? I'm not finished ironing your uniform, and I have tons of other work."

Without another thought, I yank the cord out of the wall and sweep her out of there. On the bridge, I tend to her wounds properly, applying antibiotic ointment and securing the cuts with decent bandages.

"Next time you hurt yourself—next time you need anything—you come to me right away. Don't even radio me, just come to the bridge. Do you understand me?"

She nods slowly, her eyes full of fear.

I feel like such an asshole for scaring her. "Shit, I'm sorry. When I saw you were hurt, I just lost it."

She smiles and laughs a little. "I'll be okay. I'm just a little clumsy. I don't want you to worry about me, really."

Just then, we both hear Juno's voice on the radio. "Star, Star, Juno?"

Star's sweet face blanches, and she answers. "Copy, Star."

"Why aren't you in the laundry? The captain's uniform is on the floor and looks like someone stepped on it."

I cut in, "Juno, I asked her to come to the bridge for proper first aid. She can't do laundry today; she needs R&R. Elijah, please put Dustin on laundry."

Star's eyes widen. "You can do that?"

I grin. "What's the point of being captain if I can't?"

A small, shy smile from her squeezes my heart, just as it did the first day we met. "If I'm not on laundry and not on service, then what do I do? I have to earn my keep."

'You'll earn your keep by staying off your feet."

"Oh," she replies, her face falling in sadness. "In my bunk?"

"No. In my room."

"Would you like me to clean your room again? I have to do something to contribute. I can't live on this boat rent-free, you know." Star continues to chatter as I lead her by the elbow to my adjoining quarters.

"Zip it," I mutter.

She gasps when I pick her up and set her down against the pillows. "I don't want you to clean my cabin. I don't want you touching a dish or hot iron or anything. I want you to rest. In my bed. And nobody is going to say a damn word about it."

FOURTEEN

Star

I'M SITTING on the captain's bed, the one that I made, watching dolphins swim alongside the yacht as we make our way around the cove toward the harbor in Naples. The Instagram influencers are scheduled for a shopping day today, so I feel less bad about not contributing to the workload.

While everyone is working and the captain is steering, I'm tucked away like a stuffed animal.

I tell my body to relax and nestle into the pillows. I didn't do anything wrong. I'm taking orders. Juno won't know I'm not in my bunk because they're too busy prepping for dinner.

Finally, the movement of the boat and the exhaustion of fewer than four hours of sleep catches up with me, and my eyes close, sending me off to dreamland.

When I wake, it's to the sound of someone stirring in the room. I roll over to greet the captain, but there's no one there. I'm suddenly filled with terror as a shadow disappears through the doorway as if someone was watching me and then took off as soon as they realized I was awake.

I sit up and clutch at the soft throw, pulling it over my legs. I hold my breath, waiting for whoever that was to come back, to ask what I'm doing in the captain's bed. Was it a fellow crew member or a guest looking for something? Every possible scenario is terrible.

I don't know how long I sit there like that, only that the sun has set when the door creaks again, and the captain enters the room and sits down on the bed.

He switches on a lamp. "Let's take a look at the wounds."

I can't control the trembling when his hands undress my cuts. "Are you cold? Are you okay?"

Shaking my head, I reply, "Someone was here. I think someone was just looking for you, not sure if they saw me or not."

Captain Joe stills, and his eyes slide up to meet mine. "Did they say anything?"

"No," I say. "All I could tell was it wasn't you. I'm sorry, I was just waking up."

I feel so silly that Captain Joe feels compelled to pull me up to hug me.

He kisses me on the top of my head. "Listen, don't even worry about it. The guests came back pretty tipsy from their day onshore and with a bunch of new friends. It was probably just a drunk, lost guest waiting on a drink. I'm sure nobody of significance saw you here, or they would have said something."

Everything feels better when Captain Joe holds me in his arms. He's so hard and lean, his chest strong, and my face fits against him perfectly. He's so warm and gentle, and blots out everything wrong with the world.

When his thumb scrapes across my cheek, it sends sparks of need under my skin, landing somewhere in my body's deepest, darkest parts. My breath hitches, my body deeply aware of every inch of him that touches me as he hugs me on the bed. His breath in my hair skims over my scalp in the most delightful way.

He is protection personified. As much as I know I can take care of myself, something inside needs this. Craves what he clearly craves to give me.

When he pulls back, I expect we're going to talk. When instead, he kisses me, my heart leaps out of my chest.

Every thought, every doubt, worry, and nagging reminder of where I should be and what I should be doing instead dissipates into thin air.

The kiss—there's no other way to describe it except magical.

The thing that breaks up this sweet interlude—the thing that breaks up every pleasant, stolen moment anywhere on this boat at any time of day—is the squawking on the radio.

"Maksim, Maksim, Juno. The guests are sitting down to dinner. Just a reminder, it's seventeen tonight. Eighteen, including the captain."

I gasp. "Seventeen!"

Captain Joe levels me with a stern look. "Don't you even think about jumping up to help."

"But Captain!"

"Star. If I see you serving dinner, you'll be getting a proper punishment later," he threatens.

I chew on my bottom lip, noticing how my body hums at the idea.

"Promise?"

FIFTEEN

Joe

IT WAS one of those nights.

Not "one of those nights" when you captain a supery-acht. No. It was one of those nights when you're in command of a group of Navy SEALs on the water, facing an actual dangerous enemy.

I never thought I'd see this kind of action again, but here we are.

Bratva members. Six of them. All big, all deadly. All after Maksim, for some reason.

I'll be damned if they take control of this boat, and I'll be further damned if they think they're taking my chef.

Further, I'll have Star to deal with later, who showed up to help serve dinner, cleverly masking her injuries with white serving gloves.

And now, because she didn't stay put like I told her to, she's mixed up in this mess. The gang leader, a guy called Sergei, has evidently isolated Maksim in the galley. Juno's been separated from the group. The guests were corralled into the primary cabin, and the rest of the crew is being held at gunpoint down in the mess.

I'm too fucking old for this shit.

But I do what I have to do to protect my crew.

If my head was in the game this whole time, I would have denied these assholes entry on this boat in the first place. I never would have left the harbor to give the guests the pleasure of the best sunset view at dinner.

Emotions cloud judgment. I've always known that. And now look what's happened.

Fortunately, I had the wherewithal to see what was coming and play dumb. I'd pretended to head off to bed, but secretly I'd stayed behind, hidden in the shadows, to watch these guys.

And now I'm taking them out, one by one.

No one hijacks my ship, and no one touches my crew.

Everyone who can help the guests has been separated from the group, except me. I'm the only one who can fix this situation, and I'd be lying if I said my stomach wasn't churning with fear.

On the other hand, I've dropped much stronger, meaner, and more competent characters into the drink than these guys.

I first set the SOS signal from the boat's horn on the bridge, programming it to repeat every five minutes.

One advantage of working on this boat barefoot is no one can hear you sneaking up on them. While the horn is causing no end of confusion and frustration to our captors, I manage to take each, hog-tie them, and chuck them into the tender to await their arrests.

At the end of the day, it turns out to be child's play, and ultimately nobody's hurt.

What does end up getting hurt, though, are my feelings. My stupid, stupid feelings.

I'd thought everything was settled with Star. She's mine; I'm hers. We're together. We're getting married the second this charter season is over.

But the fact that I can't grab her, hug her, check her over for damage in front of the rest of the traumatized crew is absolutely killing me.

I keep everything I'm feeling locked up until after the police come, after we all give our statements, and all the chaos has dissipated.

And then, only then, do I seize the moment to whisk Star away to my room.

"I told you to stay put. I told you...I told you," is all I can say. I had a whole speech prepared, but these words are all I can choke out.

I drag her into my lap, perched on the end of my bed, not quite sure if no one saw us disappear together after the guests went to bed.

"Captain. You know damn well I can't let the other stews serve seventeen guests on their own. Even with Quint, Andre, and the rest of the deckhands assisting. It's too much. I may not be good at my job, but I am a team player."

My forehead rests on her chest as I gather myself. I would never let anyone see me like this. Not anyone but Star. "I look forward to the two of us being the one and only team that matters in my world. I never would have let those guys on the boat if I'd been thinking."

I feel her take a deep breath like she's getting ready to say something that will hurt me.

"Captain."

"Joe," I correct her.

"I don't want to get into the habit of calling you by your first name, not while I'm working. So. Captain. Do we need to spend some time...apart? Is this whole thing too much for you to focus on?"

It feels like someone dropped an anvil on my chest.

"What are you suggesting? No. Not an option."

She shrugs. "I worry that I'm a distraction."

I look up to meet her gaze. "Your worry is unfounded."

"You said yourself you hadn't been thinking straight."

"That's not what I meant." But it's kind of what I meant. However, her anxiety is twisting everything in the wrong direction. I can't have her blaming herself.

"If anything, the moments we were separated made me even more sure of what I need to do. We need to get married; the sooner, the better."

She nods slowly. "At the end of the summer. When we're not working together anymore. We talked about all of this."

We did discuss that. We'd made the perfect plan during our weekend together at the hotel. But I can't wait that long.

"Things could have gone way worse tonight. Someone could have lost their life. It could have been you or me. I don't give a fuck about protocols. This entire charter season has taught me one thing, and that's about shooting my shot. Acting now because tomorrow is not promised."

"What are you suggesting?"

"Star, marry me right now. I know someone, another captain, who can do it immediately if I say the word. The crew will understand. You haven't been given any preferential treatment."

Star snorts. "Other than keeping my job despite being terrible at it."

I brush away a lock of her hair. "If Vanessa wanted to

fire you, she could have done that. If Juno wanted to fire you, same thing. You could even say my attachment to you was their fault; they pushed me to have meetings with you." I can't help but smirk.

"That's a stretch," she says, and I feel her body relaxing against mine. She lowers her mouth to mine for a soft kiss, but I'm not having it. I enjoy the way she gasps whenever I surprise her. I like the way she sighs and moans when I capture her lips in mine and let my passion take over.

I appreciate how she squeaks in shock when I drag my hand up her shirt to handle her beautiful breasts, teasing and tweaking her nipple.

I savor the sound of her whimpering, the feel of her writhing and bucking, the taste of her honey when I lay her down on the bed and take her sweet cunt in my mouth.

I especially like the way she comes, with my name on her lips when I ravish her like this.

But most of all, I love the way she loves me back. Even when she doesn't listen to my instructions and insists on being truly herself. She may drive me mad, but I love that about her the most.

SIXTEEN

Star

WHEN WE SAY goodbye to the gaming company mogul and his guests, the sun is high in the sky. Because this season can't get any weirder, the gaming mogul's younger sister, Ally, stays and takes a job on the crew as a floater.

No one is complaining about the extra help. Still, some other crew members seem to notice how easily Quint escaped consequences for fraternizing with guests.

We still haven't told the crew the truth about us. I convinced the captain to keep our secret until the end of the season, finally making him see that putting off a wedding is not wasting time. Nothing wrong with trying to get me pregnant in the meantime, is there?

"What has gotten into the captain? I've never seen him so permissive with the crew," I hear Juno saying to Elijah one night in the crew mess. I stay quiet and eat my food.

Elijah shakes his head. "I don't know. I've known the man for years, and I've never been able to figure him out.

He can be relied on to make adjustments when crew members are not working out, but this season? He's soft on everyone."

Juno goes quiet. I can feel everyone's eyes on me as I slurp my spaghetti. I'm not saying a word if they threaten to keelhaul me. No way.

Juno clears her throat. "So. Star. What do you think about the captain's treatment of the crew?"

I pretend to choke, acting as if a noodle has lodged itself in my throat. I make the universal signal for "choking," which I learn is the wrong thing to do in this crowd. Before I can reconsider this choice, Elijah's got two tree trunk arms gripped around my upper body, crushing upward until I feel like I might vomit. The only thing I can do at this point is to inhale loudly, dramatically, showing them that I'm saved—even though I was in no danger whatsoever.

I feel bad about lying.

Both he and Juno assess me, shining lights in my pupils for some unknown reason and insisting I fill out a report with the medic.

On the other hand, I'm relieved to be far away from wherever that conversation was going.

Before I'm even out the infirmary's door, my phone rings.

Of course, the medic had to let the captain know about my near-choking incident.

His voice sounds like he's already bounding across the boat to find me. "What the hell happened to you this time? Do I need to put a helmet on you?"

"I'm fine!"

"I'm coming to take a look," he insists.

"You could have just texted me. You do have to steer this ship, you know."

"Husbands who don't drop everything when their wives are in danger are pussies," he growls.

I start to tell him he's being sexist with that comparison and ridiculous. I'm not even in danger, but he's already hung up. I'm sticking out my tongue at the phone when I run straight into him.

"Hello, Sunshine."

"Captain!" I hiss, looking around in case anyone can hear us.

"We're alone," he says. "Everyone's getting ready to go out for the night. Everyone but you."

"I'm fine," I insist. "I wasn't even choking. I was pretending, so I wouldn't have to answer any casual questions about you," I say.

He nods, narrowing his eyes at me. "So, you were lying," he says.

"Yes?"

"I see." He's trying to sound stern, but I detect a hint of a smile playing on his lips. "Guess I'll have to teach you another lesson."

The suggestion of this rolls over my body. My muscles are tight from working to turn over the cabins all day.

"So I'm grounded, Daddy? You're not gonna let me go out with my friends?"

He towers over me. "See? I told you you were a smart girl."

Moments later, I'm in his room and forgetting the knot he just showed me. My wrists are tied together, and my body is on fire. My heart pounds like the first time he tied me up like this.

"Try to remember," he says, his voice grazing over my skin with the patience of an extra patient sort of teacher.

Is it wrong to think of him like that? Is it wrong to play

these sorts of games? I really could not care. I'm safe. This is our safe, secret, secure little cove. Just him and me.

He already seems to know what I'm thinking. "We don't have much time for our lesson tonight. But soon, we'll be completely, one hundred percent alone together for as long as we want."

I look up at him and bite my bottom lip. "As long as you want?"

The captain's brow comes together in concern. "Hey. What did you tell yourself just now? Are you worried this is a temporary thing?"

I exhale a shaky breath as his strong fingers clamp down against my forearms. I look down at them, noticing how firm they are. How those are the hands of a man who means what he says.

"I know you would never hurt me, but I can't help how my mind tricks me into thinking this is too good to be true."

The captain grits out, "Look at me."

Shyly I turn my gaze up to meet his. "Did I say something wrong?"

Barely able to stand the ferocity in his eyes, I look away again. He tugs my bound wrists upward and loops my arms over his head so that I'm hugging his neck. The captain leans in closer until his lips are a whisper away from my ear. "Listen to me. This is forever. You and me. You are mine. I'm yours. I'll keep saying it right into your ear until you believe it. Say it."

"Captain."

"Say my name."

"Joe."

"What are you?"

"Yours?"

"Try that again, Sunshine."

"Yours. I'm yours."

"Good girl."

The kiss is soft but swiftly crescendoes into something fierce and furious. He's gripping me so tight, there's no space between us.

Just as before, my feet lift off from the floor. The captain — Joe — is so easy to give in to. He handles me quickly as he transfers me to the bed and lifts my bound wrists over my head, hooking them on the headboard. The more I relax, the less the rope bites into my skin.

Seconds later, I'm surging with pleasure at the tender restraint of his greedy mouth, suctioning my nipples into tight peaks.

And I'm floating in the air in his grip. When he spreads open my folds and grinds, his arm hooks around my hips and lifts me off the bed.

My hands scrabble for purchase, helpless in their tether.

The captain rumbles against my neck. "I'm gonna untie you. But I need to ask you — can I take you from behind?"

My voice is a whimper. "Yes. Yes, please."

My wrists slip free of the ropes, and he flips me onto my stomach. I'd expected to feel unsure of myself, but something has lit a fire in me, and I raise my backside into the air and spread my legs.

The captain may completely control my body, his rough hands playing over my skin. But I'm in control of him. I look back at him as his callouses roam over my back and the curves of my rump.

"I wish you could see this, Sunshine. Oh my god."

I share a wicked smile with him.

In my mind, I had always assumed I wouldn't like this kind of position. I always thought I was built for face-to-face, intimate connection. But this is far from impersonal.

I'm completely exposed in a new way, but I don't feel exposed. Perhaps because I trust him so completely.

I twitch when he drags his hand over my damp center, then up, toying with my clit. When his opposite thumb swipes over my split, barely brushing the tight pucker of nerves there, I cry out, arching my back, pressing into his hands. I need more.

Joe crouches over me and whispers against my neck, "You like that?"

My body hums in anticipation. "Yes," I rasp.

He chuckles. "You want me to please you there, too, while I'm inside you?"

"Please, Daddy!" I beg.

"Such a polite, good girl."

"Yes, Daddy."

My beast of a man surrounds me, one thumb dancing over and around my clit. His thick shaft fills slowly but firmly. And then the roughened edges of his other thumb scrape seductively down between my cheeks and find that last, untouched spot.

An immediate release barrels through me as this man plunders all of my most sensitive places at once.

I have no strength to hold back my cries of shocked pleasure.

I just hope no one can hear us.

SEVENTEEN

Joe

"THAT'S MY GIRL. That's my girl," I repeat, pulling out and pushing back in, devastating her pussy with every movement.

My Star has learned a thing or two in my time with her. She's become more comfortable with her own body since we came together. When I pull myself out, the muscles of her sex clamp down hard around my length.

"Shit, honey. Holy fuck."

"Good?"

"You have no idea. So good, I think you might be secretly better at this than you think you are, sweetheart."

Her soft mewls in response to my increased pace tell me she's building back up to another release.

The sounds of our sex, the slapping of our bodies together, the keening and cursing — who knew I could keep up with such a fucking goddess.

My release wracks my body; I come hard and deep

inside my Star with a jolt. She's my sweet temptress, my siren. And I never stood a chance.

Later, with our limbs tangled together, I nuzzle her breasts as she sleeps.

She wakes up, giggling. "Am I your plaything?"

"You're my siren."

"Siren? Hardly."

"You don't even know," I tell her, dappling kisses over her breasts, scraping my beard against the soft, supple skin. "I'm a lonely sailor lost at sea, and I never stood a chance."

She purrs and runs her fingers through my hair. "Are you saying you latched on to the first available single woman when you realized you were lonely?"

I know she's teasing. I know she's being self-deprecating. This is how she is, but I don't have to accept it.

Rolling onto my back and hoisting my sunshine onto my chest, I correct her.

"Never. If you hadn't come along, if your soul had never spoken to mine, I would have been content to be alone for the rest of my life. I believe we were meant to be together. I love you, and if I have to remind you every day that you are worthy of happiness, that will be my life's mission."

"Joe," she squeaks.

"And don't you dare tell anyone I can be such a pot of mush. That's for you and me. Do you understand?"

"So bossy," she teases, squeezing her legs around me. "And don't worry. They already think you've gone soft. They don't know why, but they suspect something."

I mull this over before asking, "Does it bother you that we're keeping this secret?"

"I don't know. I don't think so?"

"If you say the word, I'll call a meeting and tell everyone."

"Joe, don't do that. We have to be more careful about it. We just have to be patient."

I kiss the top of her head and squeeze her close. I know she's right. Yet, something in her voice tells me she might not be telling me the truth.

I feel Star can only take so much secrecy, and I love that about her. I love her desire to live her truth.

On the other hand, I'll do anything to prevent negativity from coming her way.

Patience is not my greatest virtue. Fortunately, Star is a better person than I am.

She's my impeccable angel, and we'll announce this whenever she decides is best.

EIGHTEEN

Star

AS I RETURN to my bunk to change for a night out on the town with everyone—a fake stomach bug excuse can only be used so many times before arousing suspicion—who should be standing in the doorway of my tiny cabin but Dustin.

"Do you need something?"

He smiles knowingly. "Yeah, I do. I wondered if I could borrow a cup of sugar, neighbor."

I shake my head. "I don't have any sugar. Ask Maksim; the chef probably has some in the pantry."

Dustin looks me up and down in a way that gives me the creeps, and I just want to go get ready to go out.

"Excuse me," I say, trying to step around him.

"You're adorable; did you know that?"

My stomach rolls over in disgust. "So you've said."

"I just wanna talk," he says, feigning a "nice guy" face that I cannot stand.

I try to push past him. "I just want to get ready to go out. So if you'll excuse me."

"I think you'll want to hear what I have to say before you go out tonight with your so-called friends."

This makes me stop and stare at him. "What do you mean, so-called?"

He laughs. "You'd be surprised at how quickly they can turn on you once you break the rules."

Lifting my chin, I tell him I haven't broken any rules. Not any rules that concern him, but he doesn't need to hear that qualification.

"They might not see it that way once they notice you're getting preferential treatment."

"From whom?" Even though my insides are now roiling in anxiety, I try to sound as dumb as possible. He knows. How does he know?

He laughs derisively. "The captain, sweetheart."

"What?"

"Don't even try that innocent act out on me anymore. It's getting pretty tired. Although I have to admit, you had me there for a while. Shy, sweet Star. Dumb as a bag of hammers and clumsy as a newborn Bambi. But so enthusiastic. You had me believing you were just a simple try-hard. A little annoying but otherwise harmless."

"Does this speech have an endpoint? Because I will need an espresso to make it through the night if you're going to keep talking much longer."

He's annoyed at that. Good. I've had enough. "Sassy. I knew you were hiding an attitude behind that facade. I also know what else you're hiding. You've been fucking the captain."

I say nothing. Anything I say at this point will only be thrown back in my face. I have to concentrate, but I train my expression to be blank. Bored. I'm totally freaking out inside, but I'm not letting this turd see me sweat.

"What, you don't have anything to say to me now? No smart retort now that someone's found out your plan to sleep your way to the top?"

I should let that go, but I can't. "What?"

"You're playing the captain! You're playing everyone! If Juno finds out that your incompetent little ass isn't fired yet because you've been sneaking into the captain's quarters at night, she's going to up and quit. Moving you up into the second stew position. Maybe even chief stew since you've been here longer than Juliet."

This man is genuinely dense. That's the only word that comes to mind.

"You are out of your tree," I say. "No one would think the captain was keeping me on for certain...favors."

Just the thought of that makes me feel sick.

"No one would think that of the captain, you're right. It would be unthinkable, except for the tiny little detail of the security footage."

"What security footage?"

"After those Bratva guys tried to hijack the boat? The police asked the first mate to turn over all the security footage from that night. Turns out you and the captain had a little interlude in his room. The footage caught you together on the bridge, headed toward his private quarters. And you didn't come out again for hours."

"What do you want me to say, Dustin? Why didn't you go and tattle to your friends instead of warning me first? Oh, that's right. You don't have any friends on this boat. I didn't mean to hurt your feelings; I'm sorry."

He barks out a laugh. "The captain's going to lose his

job, and you'll lose all the support you thought you had. You're off this boat, sweetheart. Start packing."

Finally, he leaves and takes his shitty energy with him.

Juliet pops her head out of her cabin and lays eyes on me, her hair twisted around the barrel of a curling iron.

"Who was out here with you? Was that Dustin? What were you guys talking about?"

I shrug. "Leverage, I guess."

NINETEEN

Joe

I DIDN'T THINK my career would end precisely like this. With a scandal.

But it's better this way. It's better that I save Star the pain of being gossiped about. Better that I leave quietly; there are plenty of younger captains waiting in the wings, so the transition at the next port will be seamless. Star and I can disappear together before the sun comes up; no fuss, no muss.

We can go to my house in Florida. She won't have to worry about anything.

I would have liked to have captained ships until I'm at retirement age, but there are other things I can do to support us. I have my military pension, and possibly I can re-enlist as a training officer with the SEALs.

I have options, and whichever one I choose, Star and I and our kids will be fine.

What's not going to happen is whatever Dustin thinks

will happen. He left my office a few moments ago, saying that if I didn't give him my job, he would make sure I lost my license. Poor kid doesn't know the difference between his ass and a hole in the ground, which goes for boats and workplaces. The worst that can happen is disciplinary action.

But most of what I'm worried about is exposing Star to ridicule. I should have been more careful. So this is the only way forward.

I print off the letter and re-read it. Then I stuff it into an envelope, slide it under the door to Elijah's bunk, and begin packing my things.

Elijah will make a fine captain for The Carpe Diem for what remains of the summer.

TWENTY

Star

I LOOK at all my crewmates assembled around the table. Everyone is here, except Dustin and the captain.

I love all these people, and they deserve to know the truth.

Instead of joining in the lively conversation with my crewmates, enjoying a night out together, I text the captain on the phone under the table. I tell him everything Dustin said to me.

"One way or another, it seems like that kid will keep causing chaos," Joe replies to me.

I know what I have to do, but I need his okay first. "The crew deserves to hear the truth from me and not Dustin's version of events," I tell him.

The reply comes back with, "Do it."

My heart breaks, but I know it's the right thing to do. "How do I do that without ruining your career?" I ask him.

"You don't worry about that part, Sunshine. Do what you have to do. I love you."

"Love you too."

Someone's slightly tipsy laughter forces me to put away my phone. "You're distracted tonight, aren't you?" Juno says with a nudge.

I apologize for being on my phone, but I have to get everything off my chest.

First, I need to consider what to do after telling them the truth. Things will be awkward. Should I just leave quietly, go back to the boat, and pack my things? That seems like the most gracious way to bow out.

Before I can open my mouth, I hear an exchange between Quint and Elijah. "Where's Dustin?" Quint asks.

Elijah shrugs, "Says he had some loose ends to tie up."

Something about this shakes loose some memories from earlier this season, and I realize something is very wrong here.

My mind flashes back to the conversation I heard once in the crew mess when Andre and Juliet were laughing about Dustin thinking he could captain this boat. "Not with the way he ties off the stern lines. Dude is hopeless."

Then there was that other time I heard Dustin complaining to Maksim. "You're the only person on this boat I respect; both of us would like to see the captain go and let the younger ones take over."

I had grinned to myself as I walked by when I'd heard Maksim say, "You mistake my indifference as dislike. I like the captain. He's a good man. He is like a father to me."

When I'd overheard those conversations, I'd felt like perhaps he was just full of trash talk. And pipe dreams. But now I see. He's going to use this affair to make the captain quit.

"I have something to say," I tell the group. All eyes snap to me, most of them in surprise.

My hands shake, and I clasp them together over the table. "I owe all of you an apology. I know that I should be fired for being so clumsy and bad at my job. I have to tell you something. It's not just my attitude that has kept the captain from firing me. I think I've clouded his judgment and put all of you at risk. He's kept me on board because he likes me. Actually, because he...loves me."

It sounds ludicrous as I say it. But then I remember it's real. I believe everything he has said to me.

"He and I were planning on getting married quietly at the end of the summer. I didn't ask for special treatment, but we're in love. I've offered to quit, but he wouldn't hear of it. That's not fair to you guys, and I'm sorry."

Everyone's faces have transformed from surprise to relief. I'm confused.

"Baby, we know he's in love with you," Juno says.

I look from my boss to Juliet. She nods. "Yeah. He goes from junkyard dog to soft puppy whenever he looks your way."

My hand goes to my stomach, and I have to breathe deeply. It's true what she says.

I look at Elijah. "Did you know?"

He and Quint both make guttural snickers. "Yeah," Elijah says. "He's the only one who drinks your coffee. Sorry to tell you that."

So, I guess that means everyone was shocked not by the reveal but by the fact that I finally brought it up.

"The fact remains that I've been getting special treatment. I'm not qualified for this job. I'll leave to save everyone a headache over the hostile work environment I've created."

Everyone looks at each other for a moment.

Then, laughter. "Missy," Juno says, "you have not created a hostile work environment. You've done the opposite. You made the captain into way less of a hard-ass. So much so that we can actually do our jobs without getting yelled at ten times a day. We should be thanking you."

I'm so stunned, I don't know what to say.

"What next?" I ask.

Juno and Juliet look at each other and then turn to me, saying in unison, "A wedding on the beach!"

Everyone claps, everyone except Maksim.

"I'm going to have to cook another beach picnic," Maksim mutters, rubbing the meat of his palms over his face.

Juno lifts her glass and says, "Damn straight you are, honey."

TWENTY-ONE

Joe

WHEN I STARTED THIS SEASON, I had no idea the storms I was in for.

Royal drama, Russian mafia attempting to hijack *The Carpe Diem*; a surprise pregnancy, and a primary's little sister applying for a job.

The common thread is this: people have met, fallen in love, and changed the trajectory of their lives to stay together. Is that my problem? I've had one single goal ever since leaving the SEALs. I've wanted to do precisely what I'm doing. I made it. And I'm happy. Or I thought I was.

Meeting Star changed everything. She's my North Star who made me change my direction.

She is what I didn't know I needed.

Will I go to New Zealand with her? Will she come to Florida with me? We could have the best of both worlds. Hell, we could live in Timbuktu for all I care.

But I need the time to think of what to say. Call me old-fashioned, but I don't want to wait another second to get married. I want it all, and I want it right now. My wife, babies, all of it as soon as possible.

I do not know how long I sit on the dock; it could be hours. But eventually, I hear the group returning to the boat. I stand and face them, my suitcase in my hand.

Star's face falls when she sees my suitcase. "Captain, where are you going?"

Out of my pocket, I unfold a wrinkled slip of paper. I clear my throat. "I've prepared a speech. If you'll allow me a moment of your attention."

"Is this a funeral?" Juno asks.

Everyone laughs, except Star. "Don't. Don't say another word. I don't know where you think you're going, but you can't leave us."

Star marches forward, takes the paper out of my hand, and reads it. "Oh, Joe. You were going to leave without saying goodbye to me?"

"I was going to let you have some time to think it over. I don't want you to miss out on the rest of the summer, but I also didn't want what we did to cause a problem. I'm the source of the problem, so I should go and wait for you onshore."

Everyone is deathly still. Star is crying.

Finally, Elijah speaks up. "I can't take it anymore. I have to put you out of your misery, Captain. We know. We all know."

I look up at my bosun in shock. "You know?"

"We've all suspected it. You're behavior's been mega weird this season," Juno says.

Andre says, "After everything that's happened, this is honestly the least of my worries."

"Star was going to quit so you wouldn't lose your license

if we all complained to the agency about her special treatment, but we wouldn't hear of it," says Juliet.

I'm not shocked that Star would do that. I am surprised that no one seems bothered by what's been going on right under their noses.

"Oh, the agency's already heard about it; you can bet your ass."

Everyone turns to see Dustin swaggering down from the gangplank. His announcement changes everyone's face from amusement to horror.

Everyone's except Elijah.

"The captain doesn't work for the agency, though. He contracts directly with the owner," Elijah explains.

"So? The agency still receives feedback from the crew. I emailed them today, and I expect disciplinary action is forthcoming," Dustin retorts.

"Actually..."

I turn to see the first officer, James, emerging from the boat's bow and is now approaching the group. Eddie's scrolling through his phone, looking confused. "Dustin, you turned in your resignation to me at 4:45, and then you CC'd me on that complaint to the agency at 5 p.m."

"And?" Dustin asks.

"That means you were no longer an employee of the staffing agency when you filed it. Smooth move, bro," James says, a smirk tugging at his lip.

Dustin looks from James to me to the crew. "I was resigning from my position as the third engineer so that I could start the paperwork when the captain gave me his job...."

"Really?" This comes from Elijah.

Dustin is flailing now, grasping at anything to vindicate himself. "My resignation hasn't been processed yet. I'm still employed here. I reverse it! I reverse it!" He points to Star. "I saw her in the captain's room!"

Everyone is staring open-mouthed or looking away at this slow-moving train wreck.

James chortles. "Mother fucker, I processed your paperwork faster than greased lightning. Thanks so much for resigning voluntarily. Firing is so much more of a headache."

Rubbing my palms together, I try to control my glee as I explain to Dustin. "You might have had a case if you'd been using your noodle instead of ego. If you were still an employee in good standing, the agency would let the owner know about the crew's concerns."

Juno snorts. "As it is, your file has already got three, four, or five complaints about your creepy behavior. So if I were you, I wouldn't burn any bridges. You're going to need a recommendation if you apply anywhere else."

I see the wheels turning in his head. Without another word, he pushes past the rest of the crew and me, and disappears into the night.

Juno clears her throat and looks at Star with more compassion than I would have expected. "Everyone who wants to file a hostile work environment complaint against Star and the Captain, raise your hands."

No one does.

"I don't know what to say," is all I can manage to verbalize.

Juno steps forward. "Try a proposal so we can have a wedding. Or three."

Juliet jumps up and down. "Triple wedding on the beach! Triple wedding on the beach!"

Maksim grumbles. "I am not catering my own wedding."

Everyone laughs. "Don't worry, big guy. I'll pay to have someone bring food in. I can't have a groom stressing on his wedding day," I tell the chef.

I turn to Star. "You ready now?"

As she tucks herself under my arm, she says, "I've been ready."

TWENTY-TWO

Star

EVERYONE IS a little tipsy after the triple wedding on the beach, which turns into an all-night bonfire and dance party, by the time Joe makes his announcement.

And it does feel weird to call him simply "Joe" now that he's my husband. I don't know if I'll ever get used to that.

"I want to invite all of you to our house over Christmas, Joe says. "I see you all like my kids, and I don't want to lose touch."

"Weird," Quint remarks, "seeing as your wife is younger than all of us." Ally jabs him in the ribs, and Quint feigns injury.

Maksim's arm is tight around Juno; he's oblivious to this conversation and only nuzzles her neck as she pipes up. "Don't forget Vanessa. She was part of this crew, too."

"And Abel," I say, looking around at the group. Elijah, Juno, and I might be the only ones who remember working with the deckhand who only lasted one charter before bouncing. Who could blame him after a whirlwind marriage to a princess?

"Everyone is invited; I'll leave it up to you all to get in touch with Vanessa and Abel," Joe clarifies.

Andre nods and says, "We should get together somewhere every year. You all are my best friends. I have no plans to make any more; nobody understands this life but other yachties."

Juno laughs. "Yes, we will probably still be gathering for reunions when we're all old and gray."

Everyone agrees.

"Who knows where we'll all be ten years from now," says Elijah. "All of us may have moved on to other careers, families. It's all well and good to intend to stay in touch, but it rarely happens."

Everyone goes quiet. Looking around the room at all the faces, I think most of us believe Elijah's right.

But I don't know. I think we all have a greater bond than what we want to admit out loud. Everyone here, except me, isn't all that comfortable being soft and squishy on the outside.

But I know something they don't know. I believe in people. If we want to make it happen and set the intention, everything will work out. It just will.

I look at Joe, and it's as if he knows what I'm thinking. His deep blue eyes express way more than what anybody but I can see. He's a tough-as-nails Navy SEAL on the outside, but inside, his heart is fathoms deep. And so is mine.

If we say we're going to stick with this crew for the rest of our lives, we definitely will.

EPILOGUE

The following Christmas

Joe

I MADE A MISTAKE.

Everyone is in my house. So many people are in my place. So many...pregnant women.

Star finds me in the kitchen, standing in the open doorway to the backyard.

"Babe, what are you doing?"

I can't respond; I'm trying to breathe. My hands grip the doorjamb; she sees me white-knuckling it through a panic episode.

Her arms reach around my middle, and I feel her warmth against my spine. "It's going to be okay. I know it's a lot. It was sweet of you to invite them all here."

"Why is it different from when I'm on a boat? I'm at sea for an entire summer with more people than this in one vessel. It shouldn't make a difference. In fact, I should feel safer that we're all on land together. Nothing, absolutely nothing is going to happen."

Star slides around under my arm to face me, her slightly rounded belly nestled against my middle. She looks up at me squarely. "It's because we're not moving."

"What?"

"We're not on a boat, and we're not moving. You're constantly moving on a boat, even when you're anchored. When you're at home, you aren't in the middle of going somewhere else. If something happens, you can always find a way to get people to safety. You don't have enough faith in yourself, but I promise everyone here is safe. They're safer with you than anywhere else."

She points outside, and I follow her gesture. How could I forget the hired security guards stationed outside the back door? And the front door. And, at all other points of entry, the rear garden, and at the gate by the street.

I nod to the six-foot-seven bodyguard posted outside, and he nods back stoically.

I look down at the perfect face of Star, her arms wrapped around my middle. Her eyes are full of humor and excitement. I got so lucky. "I think we're gonna be okay. Ian feels bad enough about the people he hired to dig up Vanessa's personnel file and putting Maksim in danger. If he sees you panicking, he's gonna spiral."

She's right.

Star shivers, and I realize how dumb I'm being. My girl is freezing in the cool Florida December breeze. Hardly a winter wonderland, but it's a chilly enough night. I step back, my arm still around her, and click the back door shut.

We smile at each other as we hear everyone laughing raucously in the living room.

She takes me by the hand and leads me back into the room to join the party.

Vanessa is even further along in her pregnancy than Star. Ian has her feet propped up in her lap and massages her ankles. The two of them came all the way from Chicago. Ian has eased up on his travel schedule for work to stay home with her, and prepare for the baby.

I look over at Abel and Princess Angelica. They, though not pregnant, went to a lot of effort to travel here all the way from her home island in the Mediterranean. Star approaches her with a tray of holiday-themed cookies, and she takes one curiously. "When you have the baby, you should come to Austero and enroll the baby in my nursery school. I think you would love it."

Star looks at me. "Did you hear that? We should move there!"

I wince, then laugh. "I doubt your father the king would be thrilled for me to take up residence on his island, all things considered," I say to the princess.

Abel considers this. "You're probably right about that. We're all on his shit list for the foreseeable future."

Juno, seated in Maksim's lap and feeding the chef some of my homemade lobster puffs, comments, "All the more reason for the tight security. Jesus, how many people did you manage to piss off last summer, Captain?"

Everyone laughs, but Maksim looks thoughtful. He points to the spread of holiday treats. "You should consider giving up yachting and go to culinary school with me next year," Maksim says. "You're a natural chef. I don't know why I was working so hard last summer."

I take that as a compliment, but there's no way I'm going to leave Star's side or the baby's to go to culinary school. Although, it would be nice to work with him again.

It would be fun to work with everyone here again.

Quint and Ally are still planning on working on The Carpe Diem again next summer, with Elijah and Andre as captain and bosun, respectively. Elijah and Juliet are spending Christmas with his family in The Bahamas, and Andre is back home in Brazil.

"I know what you should do," Ally chimes in. "You should all chip in and charter the yacht next summer together. Give us all a bit of a break from the unbearable guests."

Some of us laugh, and others look warily over at Angelica. "Oh, I'm not offended. My family is still pretty terrible. Well, except for my sister. I agree with Juno. Let's do it."

Vanessa, the oldest of the crew, rubs her belly. "Some of us will have babies under the age of one by next summer. I'm not so sure that would be the best plan."

Angelica offers, "I could be the nanny. I'm great with kids."

"I'm not cooking hot dogs and Mac and cheese," Maksim says with a grunt.

Juno presses a sweet kiss to Maksim's cheek. "Honey, you won't be the one cooking if we're the guests."

"What is the point of being on a boat if I'm not cooking?" Maksim asks sincerely.

Juno runs a finger across Maksim's jawline. "I can think of a few other things to do."

"Get a room, you too," Quint snorts, which is quickly followed up with a playful slap from Ally.

"I have a better idea," says Ian. "I'm in the market for a new vessel. We can all charter it for free and get together whenever we want. And, if any of you are in need of a job, come work for me."

Juno remarks at the sheer enormity of that idea. "Sure. Just buy a yacht. Why didn't I think of that?"

I laugh, "Ah, just what I want to do in my retirement, let all these young kids drag my ass back on a boat."

Star smirks up at me as I rest my hand on her pregnant belly, which grows larger by the day.

"Well, this is the family you chose, Captain," she says. "You chose chaos."

She's so perfectly lovely in the light of the Christmas tree. I look around, and I'm grateful for everyone here. The panic has subsided, and all I feel is warmth in my chest. And a bit further south.

"What are you up to?" Star asks, eyeing me suspiciously.

I don't respond verbally, but I guide her into the kitchen, back her into the walk-in pantry, and close the door.

"This again," she breathes, teasing me. "You can't wait until we get upstairs?"

"You know the drill, steward," I say, kneeling before her, tugging down her maternity jeans.

"Yes, Captain." The edge of anticipation in her voice tells me everything I need to know.

I can't get enough of her. I have her naked from the waist down in a hurry, but everything I do after that takes forever.

We have no secrets to hide anymore. No rules or protocols to follow other than what we decide. And all the kids we call family out there in the living room, drinking my wine and probably breaking Christmas ornaments, don't dictate how long we take in here.

If they get hungry, there's a chef amongst them who can take care of that. If they need anything from me? That's just too damn bad. I feel as if I've raised them all to be capable adults.

As for me, the only person that dictates where I go and where I anchor is my Star. My guiding, shining, lucky, super Star.

THE END

THANK YOU FOR READING ROPED! *If you enjoyed this story, please consider leaving a review. To learn more about all my titles that are available to read, and to follow me on social media, please visit my website at authorabby-knox.com. While you're there, don't forget to sign up for my newsletter to keep up with all the latest releases!*

ACKNOWLEDGMENTS

A special thank you to Cassandra Exley, an excellent Kiwi and avid reader of romance, for beta reading this story.

And, as always, thank you to all my readers who have enjoyed this series. I loved writing it for you!

ABOUT THE AUTHOR

Abby Knox writes feel-good, high-heat romance that she herself would want to read. Readers have described her stories as quirky, sexy, adorable, and hilarious. All of that adds up to Abby's overall goal in life: to be kind and to have fun!

Abby's favorite tropes include: Forced proximity, opposites attract, grumpy/sunshine, age gap, boss/employee, fated mates/insta-love, and more. Abby is heavily influenced by Buffy the Vampire Slayer, Gilmore Girls, and LOST. But don't worry, she won't ever make you suffer like Luke & Lorelai.

If any or all of that connects with you, then you came to the right place.

Ingram Content Group UK Ltd.
Milton Keynes UK
UKHW020654050623
422889UK00016B/1593